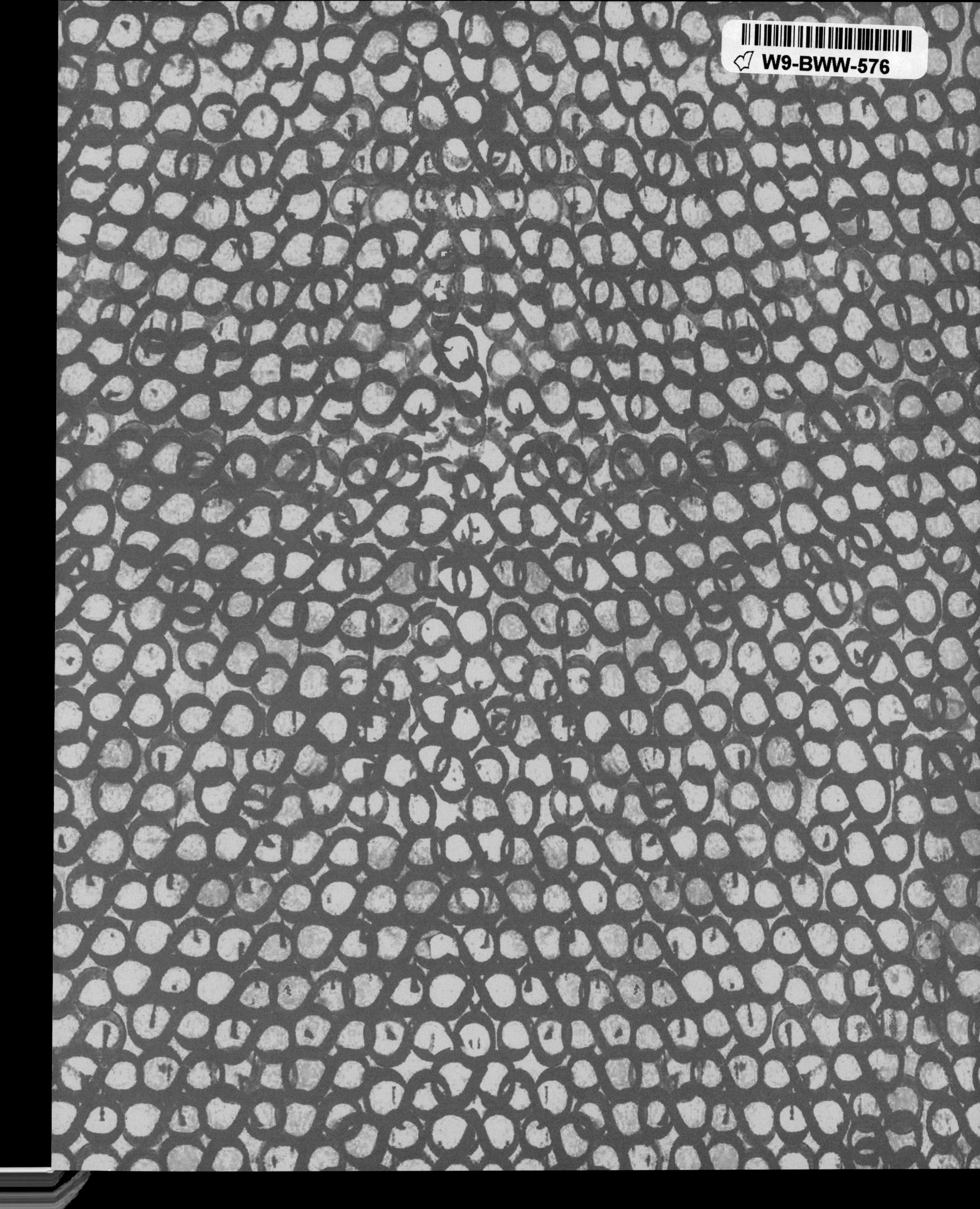

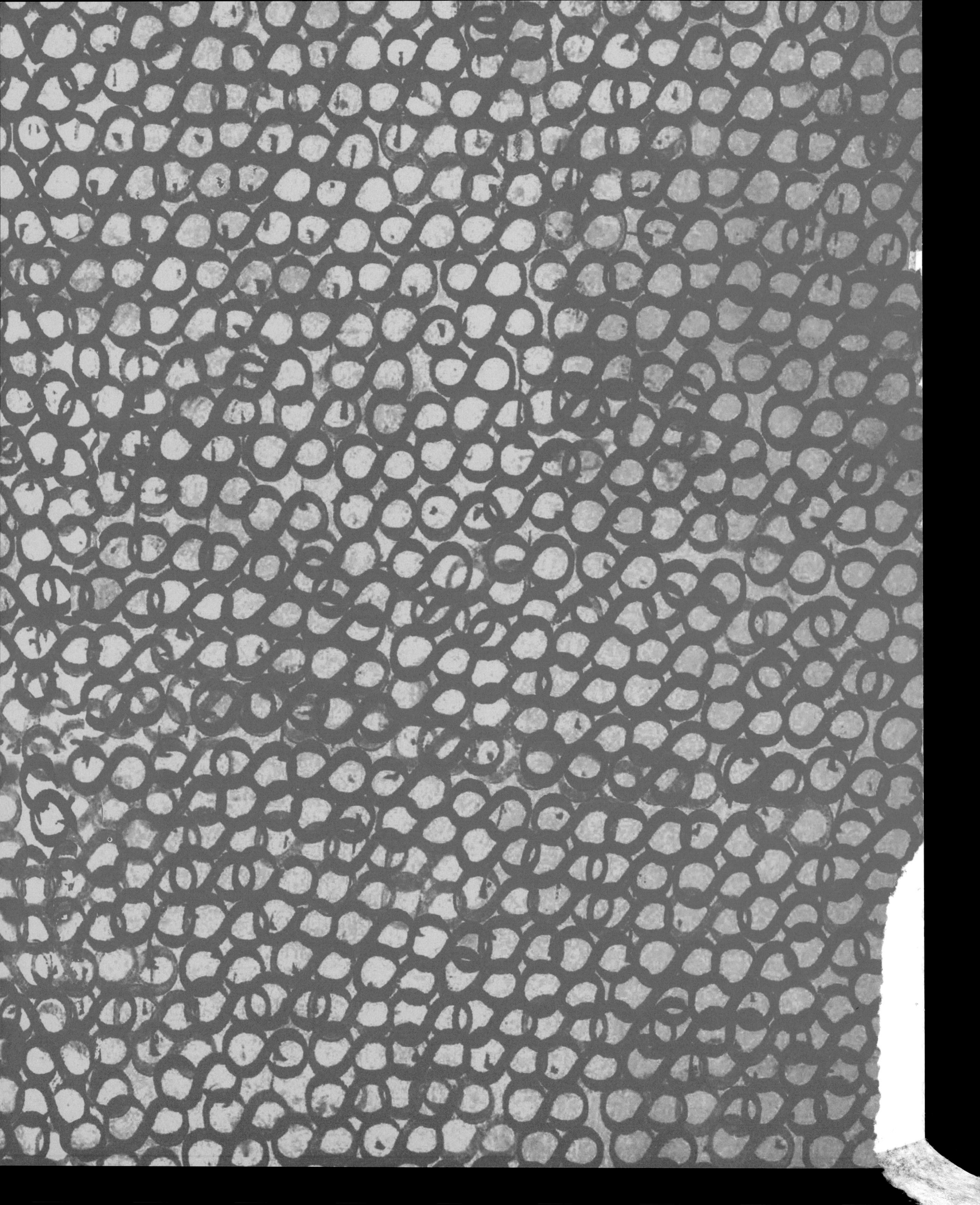

TELL ME A LION STORY

For Adam, Ayden, and Theo
and the stories we share

First edition 2022

Library of Congress Catalog Card Number pending
ISBN 978-1-5362-1801-5

22 23 24 25 26 27 APS 10 9 8 7 6 5 4 3 2 1

Printed in Humen, Dongguan, China

This book was typeset in Halewyn.
The illustrations were done in mixed media.

Candlewick Press
99 Dover Street
Somerville, Massachusetts 02144

www.candlewick.com

TELL ME A

Lion

by **Kara Kramer**

with help from **you!**

CANDLEWICK PRESS

Dad . . . ?

20 SUNDAY, JANUARY 1
THE NEW New
Story of a
story
in
a

Tell me a story!

OK.

ONCE UPON A TIME . . .

No. Tell me
a NEW story,
and make
it about
a LION!

OK.

RIGHT NOW,

AT THIS

EXACT

MOMENT IN TIME,

THERE IS A

GIANT

LION.

HIS FOOT IS
BIGGER THAN
THIS COUCH.

The lion
doesn't
have to be
SOOO BIG.

OK. RIGHT NOW,
AT THIS EXACT
MOMENT IN TIME,
THERE IS A TEENY-
TINY, ALMOST
INVISIBLE LION.

HE'S SMALLER THAN A BUTTON.

Why is the lion
so small?
Doesn't he
eat dinner?

OK. HOW ABOUT THIS?
RIGHT NOW, AT THIS
EXACT MOMENT IN TIME,
THERE IS A NOT-SO-BIG,
NOT-SO-LITTLE LION
NAMED FRED.

Fred? Why is the lion named Fred? I can think of a hundred zillion better names to give a lion! Like . . .

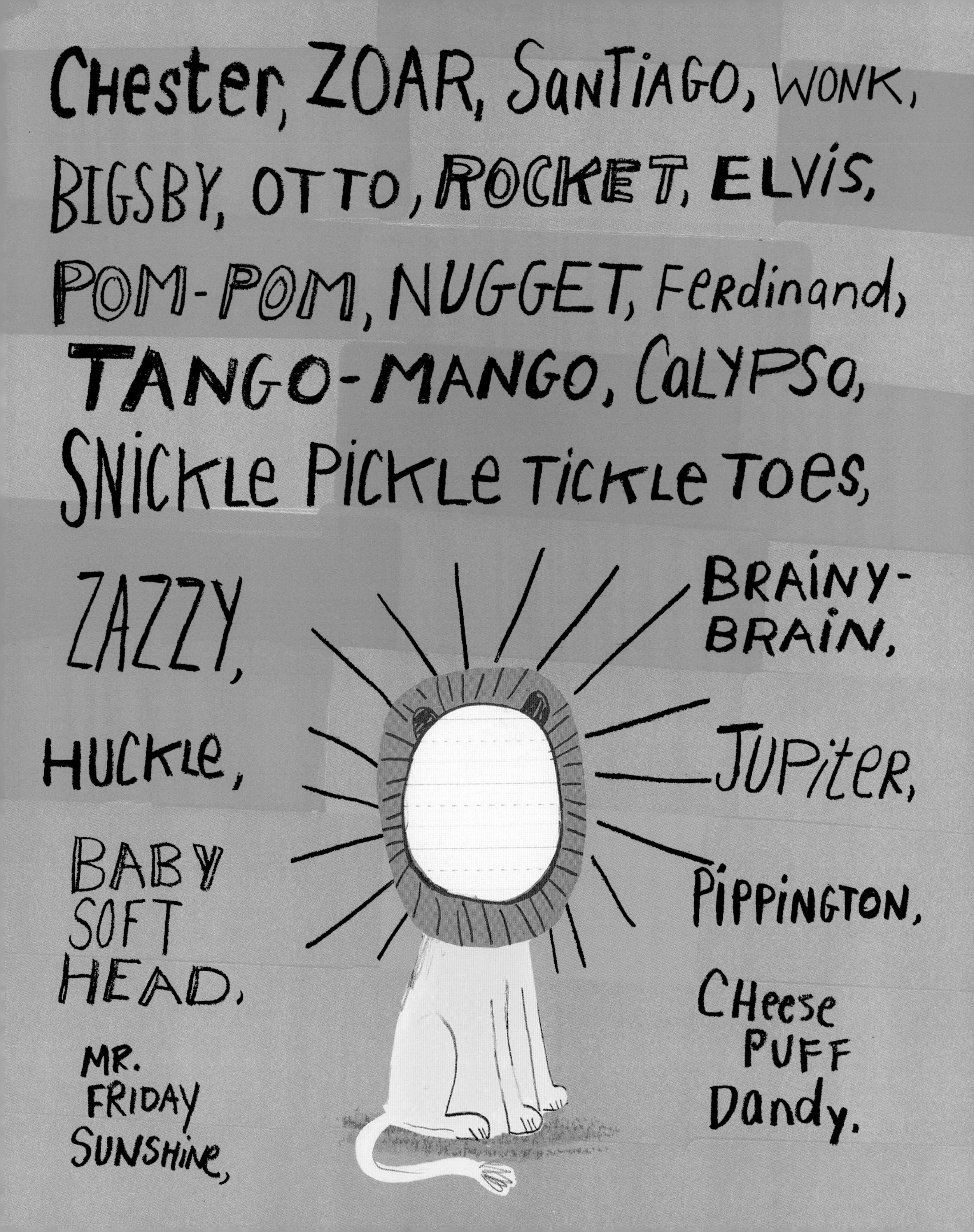
Chester, ZOAR, SanTiAGO, WONK,
BIGSBY, OTTO, ROCKET, ELVIS,
POM-POM, NUGGET, Ferdinand,
TANGO-MANGO, CaLYPSO,
SNICKLE PICKLE TICKLE TOES,
ZAZZY,
BRAINY-BRAIN,
HUCKLE,
JUPITER,
BABY SOFT HEAD,
PIPPINGTON,
MR. FRIDAY SUNSHINE,
CHeese PUFF Dandy.

TELLING A STORY ABOUT
A LION ISN'T SO EASY.
LET'S TELL IT TOGETHER.

OK!
ok

Right now, at this exact moment in time, there is a not-so-big, not-so-little lion named ________.

Where he lives there are buildings made of _____,

gardens that grow singing _____,

stores that sell _____,

and fountains filled with delicious _____.

Here, anything is possible.

With a swirl of his paws, the lion invents a one-of-a-kind flying ______!

He hops in,
adjusts his ________,
presses the ________,
counts to ________,
ROARS like ________,
and off he goes.

ROAR!
The lion flies over ________.
ROAR!
The lion flies through ________.
ROAR!
The lion flies faster than a ________.

Look, the moon!

With speeds off the charts,

the lion zigs past ____________

and zags around ____________

until he lands on an undiscovered

planet!

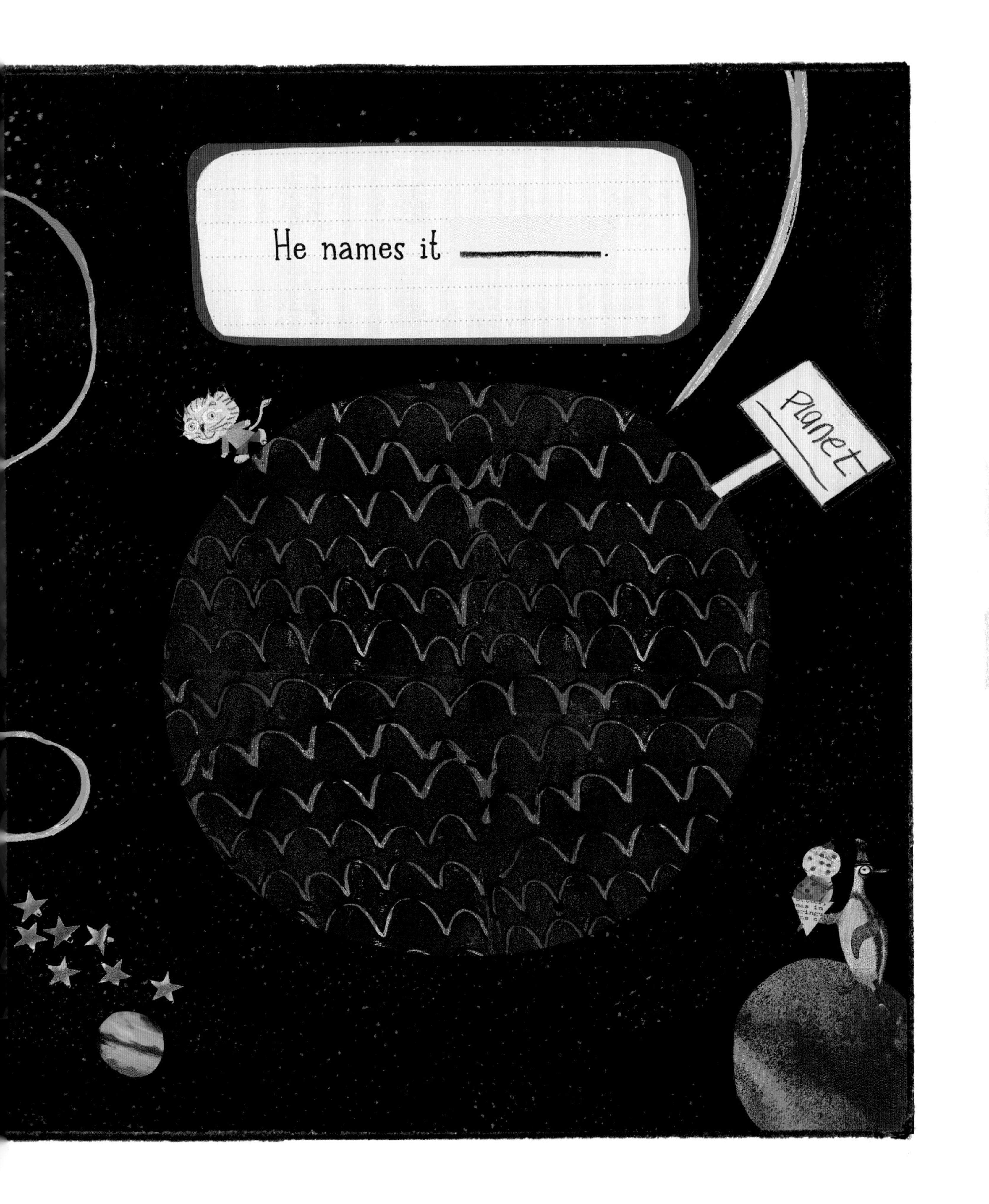
He names it ________.
Planet

He explores for hours.

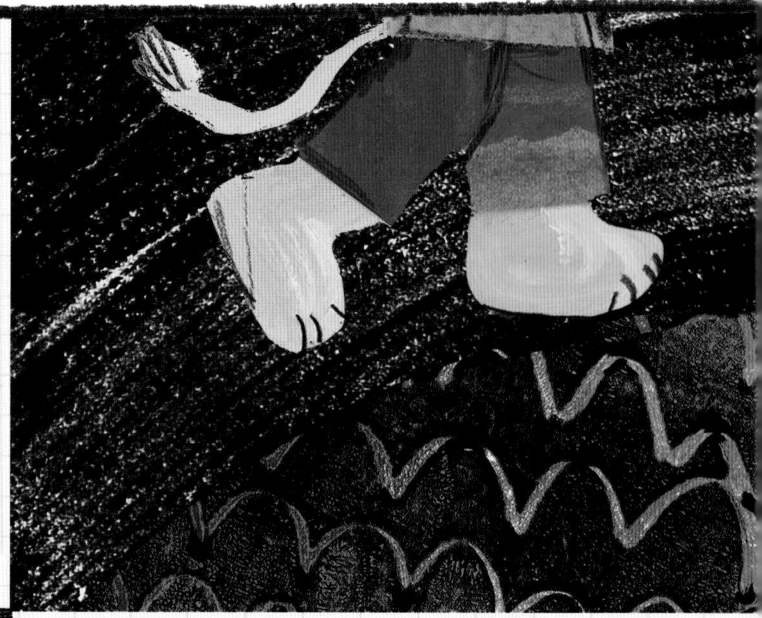

He decodes secret messages (this one says ______).

He swims in pools of ______.

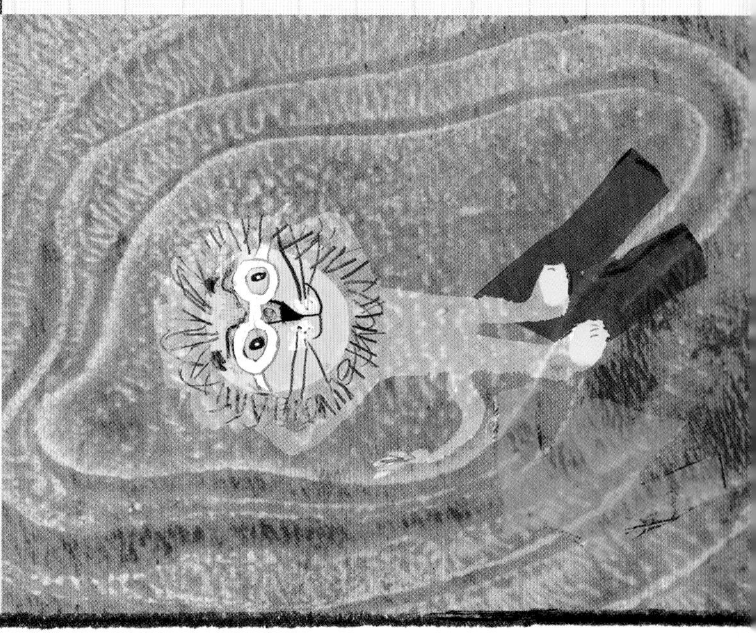

He digs for shiny

________.

He finds ________.

At last, it's time for bed.
He flies home . . .

and lands right in
his pajamas.

He lets out a yawn that sounds like ______,
then heads to the couch and says . . .

TELL ME A STORY!
AND Make it about a
_______!